Written by Meghan J. Ward

Illustrated by Tay Odynski

It was the perfect summer day,
the skies were blue and bright –
the kind of day you spend outside
from morning until night.

Instead of playing in the yard,
or riding on her bike,
Geneva packed a bag
and joined her parents for a hike.

They drove along some winding roads
'til mountains towered high.
And then, at last, they reached a trail
called "Climb into the Sky."

CLIMB INTO THE SKY

Backpacks on and boots laced up,
the adventure was underway.
A gentle breeze picked up the leaves
and pines began to sway.

As they walked, the parents talked.
They'd hiked this trail before.
They told her of the things she'd see,
they told her what's in store:

"From the summit, way up high,
you'll get a birds-eye view,

where folks below look like ants
that wander in a queue.

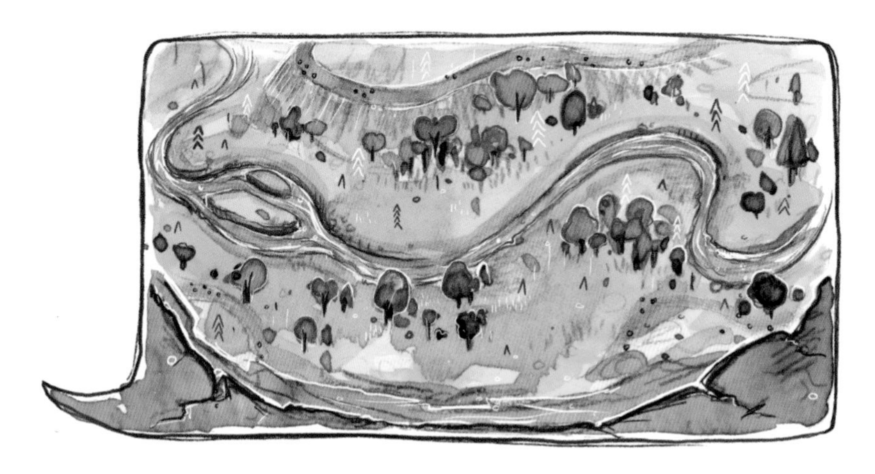

You'll see a winding river
carve the landscape like a snake.

Trees below reach for the sun
with leaves that stretch and shake.

From the top, you'll see for miles
to landmarks far and wide.
You'll see the crags and pinnacles
that form a great divide."

Soon enough the route got steep,
their hearts were racing fast.
All fell silent on the trail
as minutes floated past.

Something caught Geneva's eye
below an evergreen.

She knelt into the dirt and moss
to explore what she had seen.

One by one, ants marched along –
hundreds in a line.

Some were carrying twigs or leaves,
some needles from a pine.

"Hurry up, my dear!" her father said,
brushing off her knees.
"You won't believe the view from there,
so high above the trees!"

Time passed slowly as they hiked
their way up through the forest.
As Geneva approached a bend,
she heard a watery chorus.

There before her, a bubbling creek
had vastly overflowed.
It carved a path across the trail
and, 'round the rocks, it bowed.

"Hurry up, my dear!" her mother said.
"No time to stop and look."
She took her daughter by the hand
to guide her 'cross the brook.

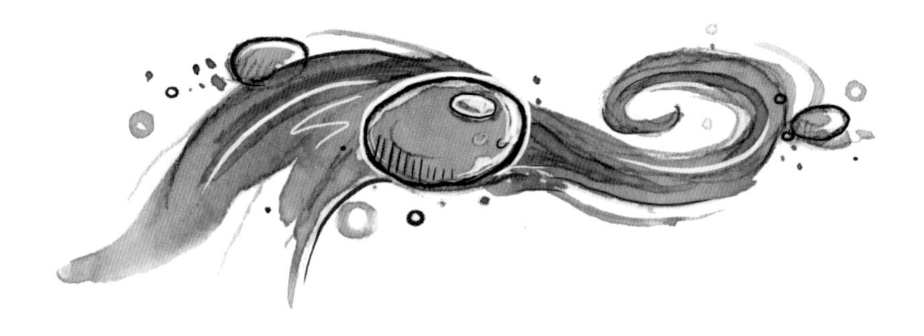

They zigzagged through the rugged wood
amidst the dew-filled air.
The path then levelled out more
and Geneva stopped to stare.

There some ferns were growing high
in undergrowth unspoiled,
'til sunbeams shone upon them
and they gradually uncoiled.

“Hurry up, my dear!” her father said.
“We haven’t got all day.”
He pointed up the hill and told her,
“Later, we can play.”

Up and up and up they hiked.
Their legs were growing stiff.
And though they had not far to go,
she paused beside a cliff.

It rose up like a wall of stone
with towers reaching high.
And on the face, so tall and sheer,
the shadows drifted by.

"Hurry up, my dear!" her mother said,
diverting Geneva's gaze.
"Our viewpoint is around that bend,
the finest of displays!"

Together they climbed into the sky

and finished the last mile.

As they touched the heavens
Geneva's face revealed a smile.

She had done it, she'd reached the top!
Mud covered both her shoes.
She stood there on that lofty perch
and soaked in all the views.

"You might have missed this," her mother said.
"That's why we hurried you.
These mountain views were worth the climb –
we knew you'd love it, too!

From the summit, way up high,
you get a birds-eye view,
where folks below look like ants
that wander in a queue.

You see a winding river
carve the landscape like a snake.
Trees below reach for the sun
with leaves that stretch and shake.

From the top, you see for miles
to landmarks far and wide.
You see the crags and pinnacles
that form a great divide."

Geneva smiled a knowing look,
aware of what *they'd* missed:
the smaller finds along the way,
the things that made *her* list!

"This view is worth the hike," she said.
"The journey is worth it, too!

I saw the tiny ants below,

the river winding through!

Ferns were basking in the sun and

stretching t'wards the light.

From miles away I saw the cliffs

that rose with all their might.

Now together let us hike back down.
More slowly, please, this time.
When I stop, come look at all
the wonders that I find."

For Mistaya Joy and Léa Claire
—M.W.

For my niece and nephews
—T.O.

We would like to also take this opportunity to acknowledge the traditional territories upon which we live and work. In Calgary, Alberta, we acknowledge the Niitsítapi (Blackfoot) and the people of the Treaty 7 region in Southern Alberta, which includes the Siksika, the Piikuni, the Kainai, the Tsuut'ina, and the Stoney Nakoda First Nations, including Chiniki, Bearpaw, and Wesley First Nations. The City of Calgary is also home to the Métis Nation of Alberta, Region III. In Victoria, British Columbia, we acknowledge the traditional territories of the Lkwungen (Esquimalt and Songhees), Malahat, Pacheedaht, Scia'new, T'Sou-ke, and W̱SÁNEĆ (Pauquachin, Tsartlip, Tsawout, Tseycum) peoples.

First Edition

For information on purchasing bulk quantities of this book, or to obtain media excerpts or invite the author to speak at an event, please visit rmbooks.com and select the "Contact" tab.

RMB | Rocky Mountain Books Ltd.
rmbooks.com
@rmbooks
facebook.com/rmbooks

Cataloguing data available from Library and Archives Canada
ISBN 9781771604444 (hardcover)
ISBN 9781771604451 (softcover)
ISBN 9781771604468 (electronic)

Design by Chyla Cardinal

Printed and bound in China

We acknowledge the financial support of the Government of Canada through the Canada Book Fund and the Canada Council for the Arts, and of the province of British Columbia through the British Columbia Arts Council and the Book Publishing Tax Credit.

Canada Council for the Arts
Conseil des arts du Canada